PLEASE WASH
YOUR HANDS
BEFORE YOU READ ME
AND KEEP ME CLEAN

Hi, my name is Darryl.

3

I live where it snows
a lot in the winter.

Before I go outside,
I ALWAYS put on mittens,
a hat, boots, a heavy
jacket, and pants. My
clothes keep me warm.

My friends and I like
to play in the snow.
That is lots of fun!

Sometimes we
build a snowman.

Sometimes we make
angels in the snow.

We NEVER throw
snowballs! That could
break a window and
hurt someone.

Sometimes I help
my mommy clean
our sidewalk.

When daddy uses
the snowblower,
I stay away.
I could get hurt.

It's fun to go sledding.

We are careful not to bump into other people.

My friend, Sammy,
lives in the country. We
sled on his big hill.

Sometimes, mommy,
daddy, and I go
ice-skating.

Mommy or daddy
ALWAYS tests the ice
before we skate.

I NEVER go on
the ice until mommy
or daddy tells me
it is safe.

Sometimes we all go skiing. That is fun!

We are ALWAYS very careful.

You can have lots
of fun playing outdoors
in the winter.

Please take care!
Remember my safety rules!

1. ALWAYS wear mittens, hat, boots, jacket, and pants

2. NEVER throw snowballs at people or windows

3. STAY AWAY from the snowblower

4. NEVER go on the ice until your mommy or daddy tells you it is safe

5. ALWAYS BE CAREFUL when sledding

About the Author

Dorothy Chlad, founder of the total concept of Safety Town, is recognized internationally as a leader in Preschool/Early Childhood Safety Education. She has authored eight books on the program, and has conducted the only workshops dedicated to the concept. Under Mrs. Chlad's direction, the National Safety Town Center was founded to promote the program through community involvement.

She has presented the importance of safety education at local, state, and national safety and education conferences, such as National Community Education Association, National Safety Council, and the American Driver and Traffic Safety Education Association. She serves as a member of several national committees, such as the Highway Traffic Safety Division and the Educational Resources Division of National Safety Council. Chlad was an active participant at the Sixth International Conference on Safety Education.

Dorothy Chlad continues to serve as a consultant for State Departments of Safety and Education. She has also consulted for the TV program. "Sesame Street" and recently wrote this series of safety books for Childrens Press.

A participant of White House Conferences on safety, Dorothy Chlad has received numerous honors and awards including National Volunteer Activist and YMCA Career Woman of Achievement in 1983, Dorothy Chlad received the **President's Volunteer Action Award** from President Reagan for twenty years of Safety Town efforts. In 1986 Cedar Crest College in Pennsylvania presented her with an honorary degree, Doctor of Humane Letters. She has also been selected for inclusion in **Who's Who of American Women**, the **Personalities of America**, the **International Directory of Distinguished Leadership, Who's Who of the Midwest**, and the 8th Edition of **The World Who's Who of Women.**

About the Artist

Clovis Martin is a graduate of the Cleveland Institute of Art. During a varied career he has art directed, designed, and illustrated a variety of reading, educational, and other products for children. He resides with his wife and three children in Cleveland Heights, Ohio.